Hugs in a Lunch Box
for ages 8-12

by Joy Stevans

Standard Publishing, Cincinnati, Ohio. A division of Standex International Corporation.
© 2002 Joy L. Stevans. © 2002 Standard Publishing. Sprout logo and trade dress are trademarks of Standard Publishing. Printed in Italy.
All rights reserved. Cover design: Robert Glover. Interior design: Robert Glover, Kurt Tuffendsam. Project editor: Robin Stanley.

Scripture taken from the HOLY BIBLE, NEW INTERNATIONAL VERSION®. NIV®. Copyright © 1973, 1978, 1984
by International Bible Society. Used by permission of Zondervan Publishing House. All rights reserved.

ISBN: 0-7847-1363-4

09 08 07 06 05 04 03 02   9 8 7 6 5 4 3 2 1

Standard PUBLISHING
CINCINNATI, OHIO

A Standard Publishing book
produced for Focus on the Family.

Heritage Builders

Table of Contents

A Note From the Author

Being a parent in the world today is a formidable task. The idea of loving, nurturing, and guiding our children into a vital relationship with Christ can be overwhelming. Sometimes, it seems there just isn't enough time to attend the games, drive to lessons, go on the field trips, check the homework, manage the home, do our jobs, and still pass on the reason we do all these things—our love for our God and for our children. I have found a small way to pass on the knowledge of that love.

I began writing notes to my daughter after I began questioning if I ever said anything *nice* to her. I got into bed at the end of the day trying to remember if I had let her know that I thought she was wonderful, funny, caring, and loving. I realized that most of the day was spent telling her things she wasn't ("That's a pretty selfish attitude") or reminding her of things she needed to do better ("Do you really think this room is clean?"). I began to search for special ways to tell her how marvelous I think she is. Then I remembered . . .

I had a friend in school who, each day at lunch, took her napkin out of her lunch sack, read it, smiled to herself, and put the napkin back in her bag. I have no idea what was on that napkin, but I have always remembered her smile! So I began writing notes on my daughter's lunch napkins. Before long, if I missed a day, she was asking, "Where was my note, Mommy?" As the notes became part of our daily routine, I realized that I was giving my daughter encouraging "hugs"—even though I wasn't with her. "Hugs" for my daughter in her lunch—a very simple idea!

What follows is a collection of some of the notes I have sent my daughters over the years. These brightly-colored messages are sure to make your child smile. If you don't have time to spend beyond just signing and tearing out one of these notes to tuck in the lunch box, you will still see the rewards of encouraging your child! If, however, you want to be a little more creative, a page of stickers has been included, along with several blank notes, ideas for theme weeks, Scripture notes, acrostic suggestions, and more!

Please keep in mind that these lunch box notes are not a replacement for your *spoken* words of encouragement, or your *physical* touches of love for your child; but they are a way to assure your child of your love every day. And the more often you think about how wonderful your child is, the more amazing things you will notice!

Ephesians 4:29 says, "Do not let any unwholesome talk come out of your mouths, but only what is helpful for building others up . . . that it may benefit those who listen." Using these lunch box "hugs" to encourage your child will open up new ways for you and your child to connect. Your child will respond in ways you wouldn't have imagined, and you will enjoy the rewards of having a family whose heritage is in the Lord.

Dear _____,
There's a space in my heart that has your name on it, and it's just for you! You are loved,

_____

You're amazing on the computer! How do you remember all that stuff?

You do a great job making things with your hands! I love to see what you can do!

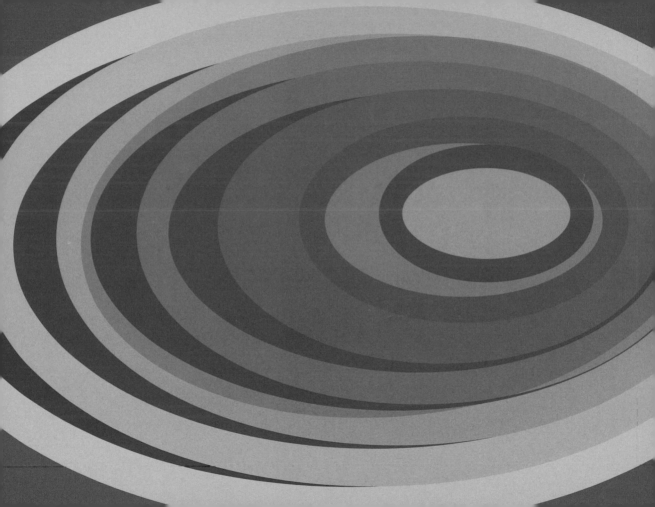

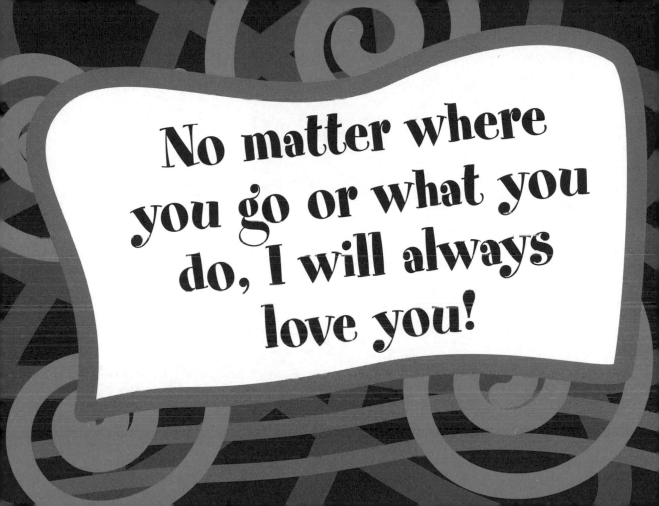

You have the best manners! I love taking you places.

You have a tender heart—and that makes you a wonderful kid and friend.

I enjoy spending time with you! Thanks for being such a pleasure to be around!

Dear _____,
You are very precious to God and to me!
Love, _____

Thanks for paying attention to what I say, even when I lecture. I really appreciate you!

You wait your turn without grumbling! Thanks for being patient!

I am impressed with the way you try to include everyone. That's just what Jesus would do.

Dear _____,
You are a true blessing
to those around you.
Let your light shine!
Love you, _____

With God's help, you can grow up to be anything you choose to be!

You tell the
funniest jokes.
You can always
make me laugh!

God made you
the way you are
on purpose.
You are an original!

Dear _____,
You do so
many things
for me without
complaining.
Thank you!
Love,

_____

Do you know that you are an answer to my prayers? You are a terrific kid who loves Christ.

It encourages me to see you with your friends. You really enjoy each other's company.

I see you thinking through decisions before you make them. That's a very grown-up thing to do!

I admire the way you show respect to everyone! Thanks for being such a good influence!

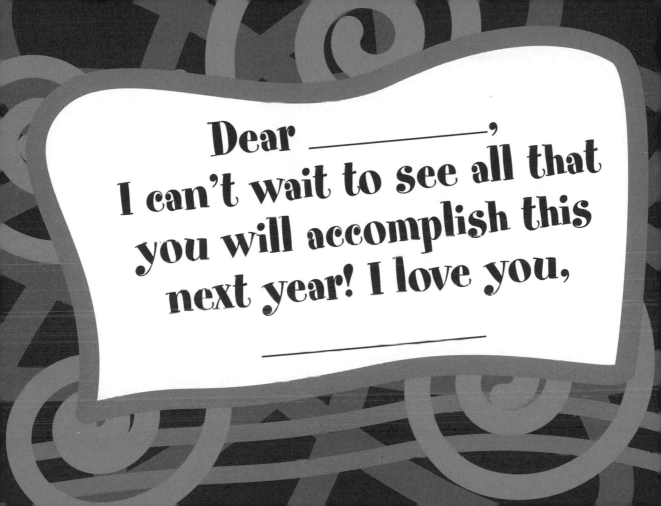

Dear _____,
I can't wait to see all that you will accomplish this next year! I love you,

_____

I always look
forward to
hearing what
you have to
say. You are
so interesting!

We may sometimes drive each other crazy, but I still love you more than words can say!

You are a great team player—at home, at school, and on the field. That's cool!

Even when I'm in a bad mood, I love you and think you are terrific!

Dear _____,
The work you
do at school is
outstanding! I'm
proud of you!
Love, _____

Every day I find new things about you that bring me joy!

If I could choose any kid in the world to be mine, I'd always pick you!

You are the kind of person I like to be friends with.

Dear _____,
I love how you listen
when we talk about
important things!
You are loved, _____

You are so amazing!
I'd like you even if
you weren't my kid!

You make wise choices with your time. You are very responsible!

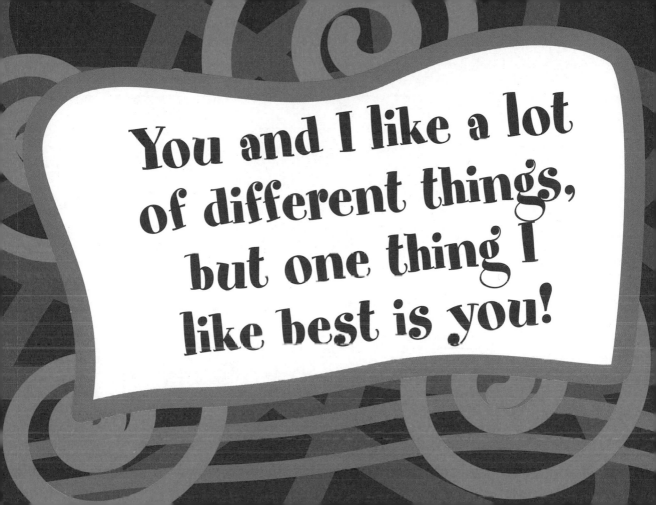

You are
comfortable
being yourself.
That makes me
really happy!

Dear _____,
I see God teaching you
new things every day, and
you are eager to learn!
Love, _____

Even when you can't do something the first time, you keep on trying—I love that in you!

Wow! You have such a great imagination. I love your ideas!

You do a good
job of making sure
no one is left out
or lonely—what
a blessing!

Dear _____,
Thank you for being
such a forgiving person.
I love you, _____

God
loves you
even
more than
I do, and my
love for you is
deeper than
the ocean!

I'm looking forward to being with you this weekend! You are great company!

The Bible says you are wonderfully made—and the truth is, you are!

No matter what happens today, God and I will always love you!

Even if you feel lonely today, you are not alone— Jesus is with you!

Dear _____,
It encourages me to see you having quiet time with God. Love,

_____

Even when I'm angry at something you have done, I still love you lots and lots!

Today will be a wonderful day—just watch and see what God will do for you!

You come up with the most challenging questions! I love the way your mind works!

It takes courage to stand up for God's truths! You are a strong example for your friends.

Thanks for keeping your room clean. I really appreciate it!

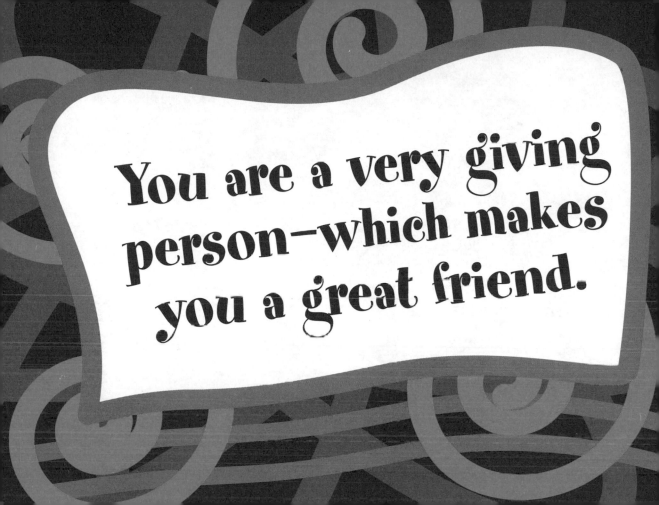

You are a very giving person–which makes you a great friend.

You do a great job saving your money! That takes a lot of self-control!

Thanks for taking such good care of your things. You are becoming more and more responsible.

Dear _____,
You are worth more to me than all the money in the world!
Love you lots, _____

You teach me new things all the time. Thanks for being my teacher as well as my child!

You write fantastic poems and stories! I'm glad you choose to share them with me!

Thanks for being patient with others; you are such a kind person!

Even before you were born, Jesus loved you and died for you. He loves you a lot!

Dear _____,
I love the way you
take care of the world
God gave us. You
make me proud!
Love, _____

Thanks for doing your homework before I tell you to. You are becoming so independent!

I really appreciate that you don't argue when I tell you something! Thank you.

I love the way you worship! Your enthusiasm is contagious!

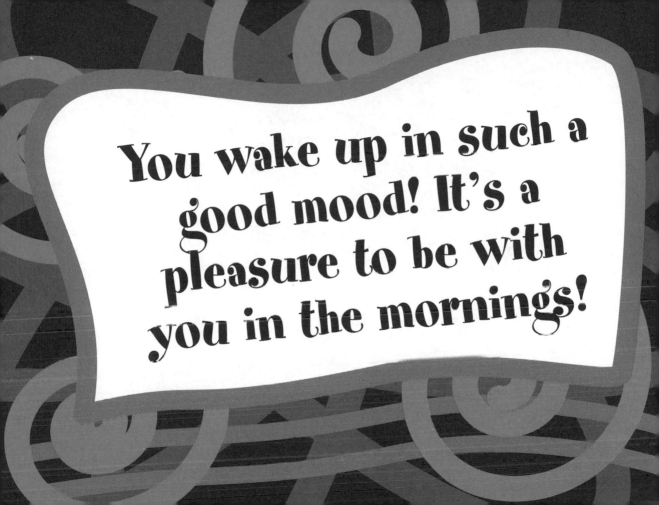

I like how you let God teach you new things every day! Isn't he a marvel?

You think up the most interesting things to do. I love watching you try them out!

You are so understanding and loving! You make me very proud!

Dear _____,
You have a great
sense of humor!
Love you, _____

We all make
mistakes when
we're learning
something new!
But God still
loves us.

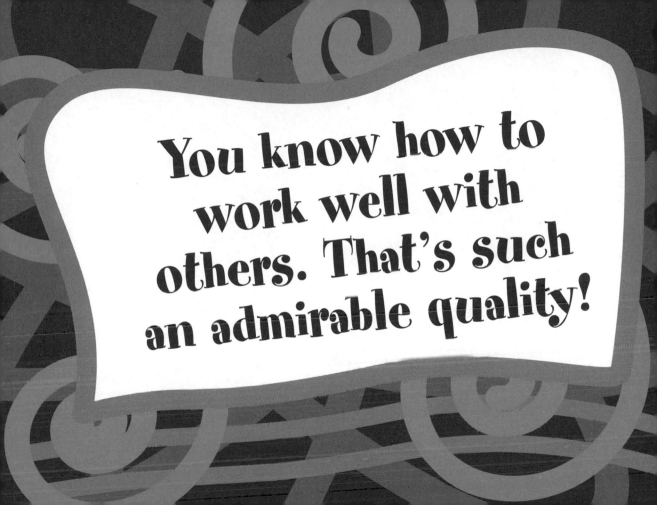

God has given you lots of special gifts. I can't wait to see how you'll use them for him!

You are   **T** houghtful
               E nergetic
               R espectful
               R eally super
               I maginative
               F un
               I ntelligent
               C ute

And I love you!

Dear _____,
I admire the way you
treat your friends; they
are blessed to have you
to care for them!
Love, _____

Without you, our family just wouldn't be complete!

Every day I watch you grow more wonderful! I'm grateful that you are my child!

Twenty-Five Bonus Note Suggestions

These ideas are great for personalizing messages to your child! Make each note relevant and applicable to her current situation. Show her that you care about what is happening in her life!

1. Today is a very special day! I will be praying for you.

2. Draw a star and put your child's name in the center.

   You're always a star to me!

3. I love listening to you sing. God has given you a beautiful gift!

4. Unscramble the letters of your message: UYO REA EICPLSA!

5. I'm looking forward to our summer vacation when we can spend more time together.

6. I know school is hard for you, but I'm really proud of the work you are doing!

7. You are the greatest ten-year-old I know! I'm glad you belong to me!

8. It's not easy to be different from the other kids at school, but I know Jesus is proud of the way you live for him, and so am I!

9. Wow! You can really rattle off those football stats! You are amazing!

10. You do a wonderful job taking care of (insert name of family pet); thank you!

11. You are a fantastic hockey (basketball, baseball, soccer, etc.) player! I love watching you play!

12. Your younger brothers and sisters really look up to you. They think you are great and so do I!

13. Your freckles are one of my favorite parts of your face!

14. I'm so glad God made you the way you are! I needed a son (or daughter) just like you!

15. I like the way you keep practicing your gymnastics; you are getting better and better!

16. Being a kid can be hard, but you make it look like a piece of cake! Good job!

17. You do a great job learning history lessons! All those names and dates might confuse other people, but not you!

18. You are a terrific dancer! I think it's great that you like to dance!

19. Have fun jumping rope today. I'm amazed at how good you are at it!

20. I can't believe how well and how fast you read! You do a super job!

21. Your decorated cookies are fantastic! You are so creative!

22. (Draw a picture of a house with your child's name coming out of the chimney like smoke.)

You make our house a home!

23. Whether you are telling a story or reciting the states and their capitals, I love listening to you!

24. Your teacher told me that you cooperate well in class. How wonderful!

25. Make an acrostic of your child's name using the adjectives at the back of this book.

For example:

J oyful
O utstanding
D elightful
I nteresting

Extra-Special Lunches

Here are some beginnings of ideas to spark your imagination as you encourage your child in extra-special ways. Remember that you are doing this for your child, so include those things that will mean the most to him. Then add your personal touches and temper your fun to fit his personality and preferences. If your child will enjoy the "fanatic" approach, then let yourself go crazy! If, however, he might be embarrassed by the hoopla, then you will want to maintain a more subtle approach.

♥ **Celebrate birthdays:** Birthdays are a BIG DEAL. Make sure your child knows just how thankful you are for the day God gave her to you! Extra-special little presents (erasers, pencils, etc.) are simply a must for the week of the birthday!

♥ **Get fancy:** Use different colored napkins—red and green for Christmas, yellow for April, a favorite color for birthday, and so on. Fold napkins as at upscale restaurants. Wrap special messages inside or fill napkins with confetti!

♥ **Puzzles:** "License plate" puzzles can be great encouragement: U R A Q T!

♥ **Wrap it up:** Wrap the lunch in gift wrap for a lunch box full of presents! Have one real gift among the others, just because!

♥ **Secret code:** Design a code to use for your special notes. Your child can have fun figuring out the code while eating lunch. Make it simple, however, as most lunch times are short and the call of the playground is strong. We have used the simple 1=A, 2=B, 3=C . . . code with success.

- ♥ **Family connections:** Include items from your family history. An old valentine of Grandma's, a baseball card of Dad's, an old report card of yours . . . connect your child to her family through little things. Remind her that she is part of a family who loves her.

- ♥ **Plan a monthly theme week:**
September: Add school supplies to the lunch box with appropriate love notes like "you add color to our home" with a gift of scented markers.

October: Spend the week telling your child about the "fruit of the Spirit" that you see growing in him. For example, add an apple sticker with the note, "You are becoming more patient every day; I see it in how you wait your turn for the bathroom!"

November: Spend a week reminding your child why you are thankful for her.

December: Celebrate Christmas! Using Isaiah 9:6 as your base, spend the week explaining how Jesus fulfills this prophecy in our hearts: "A child was born . . . I'm glad God sent Jesus to earth so we can all be his sons and daughters." Or "He is a Wonderful Counselor . . . No matter what's happening in our lives, we can always go to Jesus. Isn't that cool?"

January. Make a list of resolutions for your relationship with your child. Share them during this week. "I will think more carefully before saying 'No' to your ideas in this coming year."

February: Include valentines from members of your extended family or special friends. A surprise valentine from big brother or even the pastor of your church will be extra special. Let your child know he is loved by lots of people.

March: As Easter draws near, spend time reminding your child of what Christ did for us. Little symbols in plastic eggs are fun to get and are thoughtful reminders—a piece of unleavened bread (or cracker) for the last supper, a small piece of sponge for the vinegar Christ drank, a bit of salt for the tears the followers cried, and an empty egg for the empty tomb!

April: Plan a joke week. Come up with some of the snappy ones from when you were younger to share with your child. Include Dad's or Grandpa's favorites. Ask which ones your child likes best.

May: Have a "He is God and He loves you!" week. Explain one attribute of God each day. Although we cannot explain God in one week, we can explore some of his characteristics—he is holy (perfect); he is omnipotent (all-powerful); he is omniscient (all-knowing), he is omnipresent (everywhere at once)—and HE LOVES US! Amazing!

June: Spend a week looking back at all your child accomplished this year. "Remember when you thought you'd never get those multiplication tables? Well, look at you now! You are super!" Include special awards and certificates to really make your child feel special.

Acrostic Adjective Suggestions

Below are some suggestions for adjectives starting with each letter of the alphabet. These words are just suggestions. Let your imagination go as you discover new words to personalize the adjectives to fit your child's name and personality!

A   athletic, adorable, able, amazing, angelic, affectionate

B   beautiful, brave, bright, brainy, brilliant, blessed

C   cute, cuddly, clever, considerate, caring, charming

D   daring, darling, diamond, delicious, dandy, delightful

E   elegant, exciting, enthusiastic, energetic, excellent, encouraging

F   funny, fabulous, fun, friendly, fair, faithful, fantastic

G   good, great, gentle, go-getter, giving, generous

H   heavenly, happy, hard-working, honest, helpful, hopeful

I   intelligent, inquisitive, interesting, imaginative, important, incredible

J   jolly, joke-teller, jubilant, joyful, jazzy, juggler

K   kingly, kind, keen, kid, knowledgeable, knockout

L	lovable, laughing, little, lovely, leader, lively
M	merry, marvelous, musical, model, much loved, magnificent
N	nice, neat, nervy, nifty, nine-year-old, noble
O	outstanding, out of this world, optimistic, original, one in a million, obedient
P	precious, perfect, pretty, prized, pearl, playful
Q	quick, quiet, queenly, quality, quaint, qualified
R	royal, respectful, rare, responsible, reliable, remarkable
S	sweet, super, strong, sensitive, splendid, sensational
T	tender, truthful, talented, thoughtful, trustworthy, tough
U	unbelievably great, understanding, unselfish, unbeatable, unique
V	virtuous, vivid, valuable, valiant, vital, vocal
W	wise, wonderful, winner, warm, witty, willing
X	x-tra special, x-tremely wonderful, x-citing, x-pert, x-ceptional
Y	you're wonderful, you're loved, you're fun, you're great, you're amazing, yummy
Z	zany, zippy, zestful, zealous, zooming, z-best

Scripture References for Personalized Notes

Nothing is as encouraging as the Word of God. It is absolute truth and it tells us of God's unfailing love for us and for our children. As our children grow, it becomes increasingly important to offer to them the truths found directly in Scripture—truths they can claim as their own. Listed below are just a few of the incredible promises of God, ready to share with your child in personalized notes.

♥ **You are the light of the world.** *Matthew 5:14.* This is a reminder from Jesus to let your light shine. I love how you shine!

♥ **I thank my God every time I remember you.** *Philippians 1:3.* And I think about you a lot throughout my day!

♥ **We are God's workmanship.** *Ephesians 2:10.* And he did an awesome job on you!

♥ **Blessed is the man who does not walk in the counsel of the wicked.** *Psalm 1:1.* You have done a remarkable job of choosing good friends!

♥ **[Nothing] will be able to separate us from the love of God that is in Christ Jesus our Lord.** *Romans 8:39.* God will always love you, no matter what—and so will I!

♥ **For God did not give us a spirit of timidity, but a spirit of power, of love and of self-discipline.** *2 Timothy 1:7.* I am proud of the way you stand up for what is right!

♥ **God has said, "Never will I leave you; never will I forsake you."** *Hebrews 13:5.* You can count on God to "be there" for you.

♥ **No weapon forged against you will prevail. . . . This is the heritage of the servants of the Lord.** *Isaiah 54:17.* God will always take care of you; you can trust him!

♥ **The prayer of a righteous man is powerful and effective.** *James 5:16.* Sometimes I hear you talking with God. I'm glad you know that God wants to hear what you have to say.

♥ **The peace of God . . . will guard your hearts and your minds in Christ Jesus.** *Philippians 4:7.* Because you are his, you can rest in his peace no matter what is going on around you!

Welcome to the Family!

Heritage
Builders ®
Helping You Build a Family of Faith

We hope you've enjoyed this book. Heritage Builders was founded in 1995 by three fathers with a passion for the next generation. As a new ministry of Focus on the Family, Heritage Builders strives to equip, train, and motivate parents to become intentional about building a strong spiritual heritage.

It's quite a challenge for busy parents to find ways to build a spiritual foundation for their families—especially in a way they enjoy and understand. Through activities and participation, children can learn biblical truth in a way they can understand, enjoy—and *remember.*

Passing along a heritage of Christian faith to your family is a parent's highest calling. Heritage Builders' goal is to encourage and empower you in this great mission with practical resources and inspiring ideas that really work—and help your children develop a lasting love for God.

***

How To Reach Us

For more information, visit our Heritage Builders Web site! Log on to **www.heritagebuilders.com** to discover new resources, sample activities, and ideas to help you pass on a spiritual heritage. To request any of these resources, simply call Focus on the Family at 1-800-A-FAMILY (1-800-232-6459) or in Canada, call 1-800-661-9800. Or send your request to Focus on the Family, Colorado Springs, CO 80995.
In Canada, write Focus on the Family, P.O. Box 9800, Stn. Terminal, Vancouver, B.C. V6B 4G3.

To learn more about Focus on the Family or to find out if there is an associate office in your country, please visit www.family.org.

We'd love to hear from you!

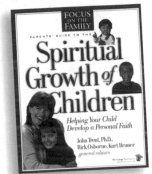